One Trick for One Treat
Sign Language for Numbers

by Dawn Babb Prochovnic
illustrated by Stephanie Bauer

Content Consultant:
Lora Heller, MS, MT-BC, LCAT
and Founding Director of Baby Fingers LLC

magic wagon

visit us at www.abdopublishing.com

For Sam, my number one favorite trickster—DP
To our Glenmorrie neighbors, whom we miss so much!—SB

Published by Magic Wagon, a division of the ABDO Group, PO Box 398166, Minneapolis, Minnesota 55439. Copyright © 2012 by Abdo Consulting Group, Inc. International copyrights reserved in all countries. All rights reserved. No part of this book may be reproduced in any form without written permission from the publisher.

Looking Glass Library™ is a trademark and logo of Magic Wagon.

Printed in the United States of America, North Mankato, Minnesota.
102011
012012
♻ This book contains at least 10% recycled materials.

Written by Dawn Babb Prochovnic
Illustrations by Stephanie Bauer
Edited by Stephanie Hedlund and Rochelle Baltzer
Cover and Interior layout and design by Neil Klinepier

Story Time with Signs & Rhymes provides an introduction to ASL vocabulary through stories that are written and structured in English. ASL is a separate language with its own structure. Just as there are personal and regional variations in spoken and written languages, there are similar variations in sign language.

Library of Congress Cataloging-in-Publication Data

Prochovnic, Dawn Babb.
  One trick for one treat : sign language for numbers / by Dawn Babb Prochovnic ; illustrated by Stephanie Bauer.
    p. cm. -- (Story time with signs & rhymes)
  Summary: Playful images of Halloween trick-or-treaters in costume and simple rhymes introduce the American Sign Language signs for numbers.
  ISBN 978-1-61641-838-0
  1. American Sign Language--Juvenile fiction. 2. Stories in rhyme. 3. Counting--Juvenile fiction. 4. Halloween costumes--Juvenile fiction. 5. Halloween--Juvenile fiction. [1. Halloween--Fiction. 2. Costume--Fiction. 3. Counting. 4. Sign language. 5. Stories in rhyme.] I. Bauer, Stephanie, ill. II. Title. III. Series: Story time with signs & rhymes.
  PZ10.4.P76On 2012
  [E]--dc23   2011027070

Alphabet Handshapes

American Sign Language (ASL) is a visual language that uses handshapes, movements, and facial expressions. Sometimes people spell English words by making the handshape for each letter in the word they want to sign. This is called fingerspelling. The pictures below show the handshapes for each letter in the manual alphabet.

Ding-dong. Time for fun!
Trick or treat. Let's count to **one**.
One warty witch.

4

one

Ding-dong. Peekaboo!
Trick or treat. Let's count to **two**.
Two creepy cats.

6

two

Ding-dong. Can't scare me!
Trick or treat. Let's count to **three**.
Three scary skeletons.

three

Ding-dong. Howl and roar!
Trick or treat. Let's count to **four**.
Four wild werewolves.

four

Ding-dong. They're alive!
Trick or treat. Let's count to **five**.
Five moaning mummies.

five

Ding-dong. **Play some tricks!**
Trick or treat. Let's count to six.
Six playful pumpkins.

14

six

Ding-dong. Is this heaven?
Trick or treat. Let's count to **seven**.
Seven zany zombies.

16

seven

Ding-dong. Getting late!
Trick or treat. Let's count to **eight**.
Eight spooky spiders.

18

eight

Ding-dong. **Screech and whine!**
Trick or treat. Let's count to nine.
Nine ghastly ghosts.

20

nine

Ding-dong. **Ring again!**
Trick or treat. Let's count to ten.
Ten haunted houses.

ten

Ding-dong. **Almost done!**
Let's count down from ten to one.

count

Ten haunted houses. Nine ghastly ghosts.
Eight spooky spiders. Seven zany zombies.
Six playful pumpkins.

Five moaning mummies. Four wild werewolves.
Three scary skeletons. Two creepy cats.
One warty witch.

American Sign Language Glossary

Numbers can be signed with either the right or left hand. Most people sign numbers with the hand they use to hold a pencil. This is called the dominant or active hand. Some people sign the numbers 1-5 with the palm facing out toward the person who is being signed to. This is how the pictures are shown in this book. Other people prefer to sign the numbers 1-5 with the palm facing in toward the person who is doing the signing.

one, 1: Use your thumb to bend your last three fingers into the palm of your hand. Your pointer finger should point up.

two, 2: Use your thumb to bend your last two fingers into the palm of your hand. Hold your first two fingers apart and point them up. Your first two fingers should make the same shape as the letter *V*.

three, 3: Bend your last two fingers down toward the palm of your hand. Hold your first two fingers apart and point them up. Stretch your thumb out to the side.

four, 4: Spread all four fingers apart and point them up. Bend your thumb at the large knuckle so it rests in your palm.

five, 5: Spread all four fingers and your thumb apart. Your fingers should point up and your thumb should point slightly to the side.

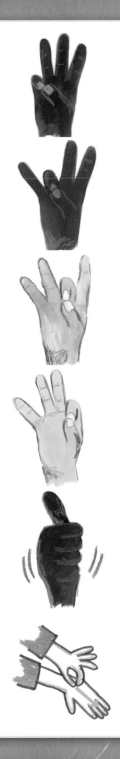

six, 6: Curve your pinkie finger down toward your thumb until your fingertip touches the tip of your thumb. Point up with your first three fingers. Note: Your middle finger may lean slightly back toward your body.

seven, 7: Curve your third finger (your "ring finger") down toward your thumb until your fingertip touches the tip of your thumb. Point up with your other three fingers.

eight, 8: Curve your second finger (your "middle finger") down toward your thumb until your fingertip touches the tip of your thumb. Point up with your other three fingers.

nine, 9: Curve your pointer finger down toward your thumb until your fingertip touches the tip of your thumb. Point up with your last three fingers. Note: Your middle finger may lean slightly forward and away from your body.

ten, 10: Hold your "A Hand" in front of you with your thumb pointing up. Now quickly twist your hand from side to side a couple of times.

count: Touch the pointer finger and thumb of your right "F Hand" to the palm of your left hand near your wrist. Now slide your pointer finger and thumb across the palm of your left hand until you reach your fingertips. It should look like you are counting small objects that are lined up on the palm of your hand.

Fun Facts about ASL

If you sign numbers with your palm facing out toward the person being signed to, you will notice that some number signs are the same as some letter signs. For example, the signs for *two* and *V* use the same handshape. Usually the context will clarify if you are signing a number or a letter, but if you want to be sure to avoid confusion, you can sign the numbers 1 through 5 with your palm facing in toward you.

One way to tell someone how old you are is to point to your chin, then sign the number for your age. Another way is to use the sign for *old* by making a fist near your chin. Now move your fist down and out as you sign the number for your age.

Learning the signs for the numbers 1 to 10 can help you make the signs for other words. For example, to make the sign for mother, you tap the thumb of your "Five Hand" on your chin. This is similar to how the alphabet handshapes are used to describe many other signs. For example, in the glossary of this book you will see that the "A Hand" is used when you make the sign for the number 10.

Signing Activities

Count and Hop Circle Game: Stand in a circle and choose someone to go first. The first player makes the sign for the number *one*. The second player makes the sign for the number *two*. Play continues with each player making the sign for the next number in sequence all the way up to ten. The player that signs *ten* must hop in place anywhere between one and five times then sits down. The player that goes next must start counting with the next number. So, if the player before him or her hops five times, the next player would make the sign for *six*. Play continues until everyone is sitting down.

Sign Language Math Fun: This is a fun game for partners. On the front of 24 blank index cards, use the digits 1 through 9 to write a math equation that equals a number between 1 and 10. For example, on the first card, write $1 + 1 = \ ?$ Put the answer, for example, $1 + 1 = 2$, on the back of each card. Shuffle the 24 cards and lay them in a pile, with the answers facing down. When it is your turn, draw a card from the pile and calculate the answer. Use a number sign to show your answer to your partner. If you get the correct answer and show the correct sign, keep the card. If you make a mistake, put the card at the bottom of the pile. Take turns with your partner until all the cards have been used and correctly answered at least once.

Additional Resources

Further Reading

Coleman, Rachel. *Once Upon a Time* (Signing Time DVD, Series 2, Volume 11). Two Little Hands Productions, 2008.

Edge, Nellie. *ABC Phonics: Sing, Sign, and Read!* Northlight Communications, 2010.

Heller, Lora. *Sign Language for Kids*. Sterling, 2004.

Valli, Clayton. *The Gallaudet Dictionary of American Sign Language*. Gallaudet University Press, 2005.

Web Sites

To learn more about ASL, visit ABDO Group online at **www.abdopublishing.com**. Web sites about ASL are featured on our Book Links page. These links are routinely monitored and updated to provide the most current information available.